DISNEP

Herbie FULLY LOADED

The Junior Novelization

Adapted by Irene Trimble

Story by Thomas Lennon & Robert Ben Garant
and Mark Perez

Screenplay by Thomas Lennon & Robert Ben Garant
and Alfred Gough & Miles Millar

Produced by Robert Simonds

Directed by Angela Robinson

Still photography by Richard Cartwright

Random House 🏠 New York

53

The Junior Novelization

This is a work of fiction. Names, characters, places, and incidents either are the product of the author's imagination or are used fictitiously. Any resemblance to actual persons, living or dead, events, or locales is entirely coincidental.

53

Chapter
1

The sun sparkled on the sand of Venice Beach as Maggie Peyton whipped through the people on the boardwalk. Her red hair blew in the wind as she picked up speed on her skateboard.

She expertly railslid down a steep staircase into a concrete pipeline. Loving every moment, she shot back out into the sunshine. She almost forgot why she was in such a hurry. She checked her watch as she took a sharp left and headed down a neatly landscaped path. Maggie could see a huge crowd gathered ahead of her at the far end of the path.

Maggie pulled a hair tie from her backpack. Quickly, she put her hair up in a casual bun and popped in two earrings. Digging deeper into her pack, she grabbed a sensible cardigan sweater to complete the look.

As she neared the crowd, Maggie heard the echo of names being called from a loudspeaker.

". . . Hillary Peterson . . ."

"Curt Pennington . . . Amy Peters . . ."

"Maggie Peyton."

In a flash, Maggie yanked her graduation gown out of the pack and threw it on. She flipped her graduation cap onto her head and tucked her board under her arm.

Maggie stepped effortlessly onto the stage and received her college diploma. She scanned the crowd for her dad. He wasn't hard to find in his bright blue Team Peyton racing jacket. Ray Peyton senior raised his camera and clicked off a shot. He was grinning from ear to ear.

Spotting his daughter in the crowd after the ceremony, Ray Peyton senior shook his head with the same wide grin stretched across his face.

"I've seen some photo finishes in my day, but that was cutting it close!" he said, wrapping his arms around his daughter and giving her a giant bear hug.

"Okay, Dad," Maggie gasped, "oxygen deprived. Getting dizzy."

Ray senior stepped back and smiled.

"Your mom would have been so proud of you today, spark plug. The first Peyton to graduate college."

"At least one where you don't get to keep the toolbox at the end," Maggie said, looking around for her brother. "Where's Ray junior?"

"Running laps," her dad answered. "We've got to perform better in the race next week, and he just doesn't seem ready for the track yet."

"My brother put his stock car ahead of his sister's graduation," Maggie said with feigned melodrama. Racing had always come first in the Peyton family. "But I'm sure the emotional scars will eventually heal."

Maggie suddenly heard the rapid-fire voice of her best friend, Charisma, behind her. "Check out my graduation gift," she was squealing. "It's a hybrid!"

Old man Peyton made a sour face.

Maggie laughed.

"My father the fossil fuel depleter," she said,

giving him a playful elbow to the ribs.

"It's good to see you, Charisma," Ray senior said. "Promise you'll keep an eye on Maggie in New York."

"Oh please. We'll be roommates for like fifteen minutes, until Maggie becomes a star," Charisma bubbled. "She's totally going to be the next big thing."

"It's just a producer's assistant job at ESPN," Maggie said, trying to play it down. "With emphasis on 'assistant.'"

Charisma shook her head at Maggie and stated the obvious. "You like sports, you're a girl, and you're hot. You don't need two degrees in physics, which I have, to know that you'll be in front of the camera in a heartbeat."

She gave Maggie a hug and climbed into her new baby blue hybrid.

"Have a great time in Paris," Maggie called to her friend.

"Be back in a month, and then I'll spring you from Riverside. We'll road-trip to the Big Apple and start our new lives," Charisma said as she gunned the engine of the little car. "Don't forget your half of the first and last months' rent and the security deposit on the apartment."

Maggie smiled and tried to hide her panic. "I'll have it," she said, as if it were nothing to worry about.

"*Au revoir*," Charisma yelled as she roared away.

"The French aren't gonna know what hit them," Ray senior said flatly. Then he checked his watch. "Come on," he said to Maggie. "I promised your brother I'd make it to the track as soon as I could."

"Wait," Maggie called to her dad as he hurried off. "Don't I even get a graduation lunch?"

Chapter 2

Maggie looked down at a tray piled with hot dogs, French fries, soda, and churros. The sound of cars zooming down the track filled the air. Maggie sighed.

"This isn't quite what I had in mind," she said to her father as they headed down into the grandstand.

"Hey, I sprang for the churros, didn't I?" Ray senior said, smiling as they took their seats.

Maggie scanned the pack for her brother's car. The cars on the track were doing one hundred and thirty miles per hour. The roar was deafening.

Maggie suddenly spotted a woman wearing a Bass Pro jacket in the stands.

"Hey, is Sally still sponsoring you?" she asked her dad, pointing at the woman.

"One of the few, the proud." Ray senior smiled

as they stood up and walked toward Sally.

"Congrats on the ESPN job," Sally said to Maggie, giving her a hug.

"I was thinking Maggie could swing us some free publicity," Ray senior said, looking proudly at his daughter.

"The only publicity Team Peyton needs is to win a race," Sally teased, gently poking him in the chest with her finger.

"Tell the boys at Bass Pro to keep the faith. Things are going to turn around. I know it," old man Peyton said as optimistically as ever.

Maggie shouted as her only brother, Ray junior, began to move up in the pack.

"Take it easy, Ray! You're pushing that right front tire too hard!"

Suddenly, Ray's car swerved. His tire blew, sending him skidding down the track sideways.

Maggie gasped and shouted, "Hold her steady or she'll—"

But it was too late. Ray's car, number 86, flipped, somersaulted across the track, and crashed into the fence in a shower of sparks.

Maggie held her breath. Miraculously, Ray climbed out of the smoking wreck unhurt. The crowd stood up and cheered! They were as relieved and excited as Maggie was to see that Ray was alive and well.

Ray looked up, and there was Maggie in front of him in the grandstand. "You were pushing the right front too hard, Ray," she shouted.

Ray was furious. He repeated sarcastically, *"You were pushing the right front too hard, Ray."*

He threw his helmet down in disgust. The only thing he hated more than losing was having his sister tell him what he'd done wrong.

"Say what you want; he loses with style," Maggie said as she watched her brother storm toward the pit.

"He's sure had enough practice," Sally agreed.

Chapter 3

Charred and dented, old car number eighty-six was towed into the pit.

"How's she look, Augie?" Ray junior asked Team Peyton's mechanic.

"Fine," Augie answered, sticking his head out from under the hood. "*Real* fine. Course it's kinda hard to tell from here."

Ray suddenly saw the faraway look in the young mechanic's eyes, then realized what he was really looking at. Maggie was walking toward Team Peyton's pit bay.

"Keep your eyes *in*, Augie," Ray said, smacking him in the head. "That's my sister!"

As Maggie walked past the pit crew mechanics, she made eye contact with the bad boy of racing himself, the arrogant but beautiful Trip Murphy.

Trip was surrounded by three little kids wearing Make-A-Wish T-shirts. He gave Maggie a wink as she passed.

"Your boyfriend's in the next bay . . . ," Ray said to his sister as she walked toward him.

"Shut up!" she barked. "I had a crush on Trip Murphy when I was like thirteen."

Ray laughed. "Remember you had to hang his poster in your closet so Dad wouldn't see it?"

Maggie stuck out her tongue at her brother. "I missed you, too, Ray." Then she said sweetly to old car 86, "But I missed you more. Poor baby! What did he do to you?"

Ray rolled his eyes. "Whatever you're going to say—don't."

Maggie picked up a hydraulic wrench. "I wouldn't want to give advice when it's not wanted—but your right rear spring is way too soft and that's why you were pushing."

"Stay away from that car," Ray warned her. She raised the wrench over her head as he tried to take it out of her hand, just as he had done when they were kids.

Maggie and Ray tumbled into a rack of tires.

Unfortunately, at that moment, Trip Murphy was doing a live TV interview in the next bay. He had his arms around the Make-A-Wish kids.

"Trip, what do you love most about being a Cup Series champion?" the interviewer asked.

Trip flashed a Hollywood smile. "It's the inspiration it gives to kids like Neil, Matt, and Tanya here. It lets them know it's okay to dream."

Suddenly, the rack of tires toppled onto Trip's gleaming stock car.

The camera quickly shifted to Maggie lying on the floor. "I'm—I'm so sorry," she stammered.

"I'm sure we can let it slide this time," Trip said, giving Maggie a smile. "You want to tell all the folks at ESPN your name?"

"ESPN?" Maggie said, horrified.

"It's a special they're filming," Trip said. "'Invincible: A Week in the Life of Trip Murphy.'"

Maggie felt like a deer in the headlights as the camera moved closer. "Uh, I'm . . . um . . . Maggie Peyton."

"Ray's sister?" Trip asked. "I remember you hanging out in the pit when your dad was still racing. You're all grown up."

Trip motioned the camera guys to back off.

He looked over at Ray's mangled car. "Too bad about Ray. He's a great guy, but the racing gene must have skipped a generation."

Trip began to laugh. "I got stuck behind him on lap one-fifty-two in Talladega; took a couple of seconds off my time. My crew's got a nickname for him." Trip turned to his pit boss. "What is it again, Crash?"

Crash smirked. "In the Way Ray," he answered, making the rest of Trip's pit crew chuckle.

Trip laughed. "Oh, man, that's harsh!"

"If you're gonna insult me, then insult me to my face," Ray said, stepping up to his rival.

"Hey, everyone can use a little constructive criticism," Trip said, taunting Ray junior with a sympathetic shrug.

Ray junior's temper flared. Trip and Crash took a step back, but Maggie stepped between them and her brother.

"Okay, Trip," Ray senior said, walking into the middle of the confrontation. "Take your traveling circus somewhere else. We'll settle our differences on the track."

Trip turned to Maggie and winked. "Whatever you say, Mr. Peyton. You know, I have nothing but respect for you. I just feel bad that you've got to watch your family dynasty go down in flames."

Trip and Crash watched as Maggie and her dad climbed into the old Team Peyton pickup and Ray junior stomped back to number 86. Maggie closed her eyes. It had been a long day.

Driving in the truck, Maggie turned to her dad as they passed a huge old tree that grew at an odd angle. Maggie gritted her teeth. "You drove past that tree on purpose," she told him.

Old man Peyton shrugged. "It's a shortcut."

Maggie nodded. "I thought you were going to cut it down."

"You hit it at one hundred miles per hour. You think I could take it down with an axe?"

Maggie stared out the window at the gnarled old tree. "I just wish my stupidest moment wasn't immortalized in tree bark."

"I don't blame you; I blame . . . what's his name?"

"Kevin," Maggie answered. "And it wasn't his fault. He was my mechanic. I entered the race. I crashed the car."

"Maggie, that's ancient history. The important thing is that you're alive and well and leaving this town in your rearview mirror."

(53)

Chapter
4

Maggie carried her backpack up the stairs to her old room. "Aw, man," she said to herself as she looked around. Team Peyton T-shirts and baseball caps were piled up all over the room.

She opened her closet, and an avalanche of wrench-wielding teddy bears fell out. "C'mon!" Maggie shouted as the little bears toppled from a top shelf.

Maggie had hoped they weren't using her room as storage, but the teddy bears left no doubt. She boxed up a bunch of them along with the T-shirts and carried them down to the den.

Maggie set the box down in front of the family trophy case and a wall of framed and tacked or taped up old newspaper clippings. She stared at a clipping of her grandfather. He was lying on a stretcher, holding a first-place trophy and grinning from ear to ear. "Now, *you*, Gramps, had style," Maggie said, tapping the glass.

"He certainly did," Ray senior agreed as he walked into the den.

"I'm sorry about not pulling out all the stops for your graduation," he told her. "That was always Mom's department."

Maggie smiled, then looked at him seriously. "I had no idea the team was doing so badly," she said to her father. "Ray said you took out another mortgage on the house. You should have told me."

Old man Peyton shrugged it off with a laugh. "We'll pull it out. It's just a bad streak. There's always another race."

He looked at all the old trophies and clippings. He held up Maggie's diploma and smiled.

"I think it's time we made a space for you up here," he said, tacking it to the Peyton family's wall of pride. "That ought to do it justice."

Maggie smiled too and kissed him on the cheek. "Night, Dad."

"I wanna get you a graduation present," Ray senior called to her as she headed up the stairs.

"I don't need anything."

"Gifts aren't about need," he said. "Tomorrow morning, bright and early, you can pick it out."

Maggie couldn't help feeling a little excited. She thought about Charisma's graduation present. Maybe it was her turn!

Chapter
5

The next day, Maggie found herself staring into a wasteland of rusted old cars. "Dad, what are we doing here?"

She looked up at the battered sign: BUMPER BONANZA—WE CRUNCH PRICES!

Her father put his arm around her and grinned. "Getting you a car!" he announced proudly.

Maggie sighed. "I appreciate the gesture, Dad, but I'm only going to be home a month."

"And I can't chauffeur you around," Ray senior added.

Maggie rolled her eyes. She kicked the tire of one wreck, then looked through the broken windshield of another. She sighed, then spotted something interesting. It was a rusted stock car.

Maggie walked toward the stock car, passing a little 1963 Volkswagen Beetle. In the junkyard, the

18

car was all but forgotten, but once it had been a champion. It had been white, but now it was covered with rust, dirt, and graffiti. Maggie did not know that the little car had once had a name: Herbie.

Herbie's rear brake light began to glow softly as he watched Maggie run her finger over the hood of the stock car.

Maggie got behind the wheel of the stock car and for a moment pretended she was racing. "One lap to go and Maggie Peyton is about to make racing history!" she said out loud, gripping the wheel.

Herbie watched as Maggie mimicked the roar of the crowd.

"And she's done it!" Maggie cheered. "Unbelievable! The first female driver to take the cup!"

Herbie's taillights glowed even more brightly. Herbie was sure that she was the one he had been waiting for. He liked her a lot.

"Maggie," Ray senior, called out, "you find anything?"

Maggie jumped out of the stock car. "Not yet. Still looking."

Herbie tried to roll toward Maggie as she walked

away, but with no rear tires, he simply fell off his blocks.

As Maggie searched for anything that looked as if it might run, the sound of a giant crane filled the yard. An old Pontiac was being dropped into the crusher. The Pontiac was flattened, then pressed into a cube by the jaws of the giant machine.

Herbie's headlights watched the car being crunched. He was next in line.

"Any luck?" Maggie's dad asked her.

Maggie shook her head.

"Nothing's calling out to me," she yelled back as little Herbie began to panic. The crane was looming over him.

"Trust me," Dave, the owner of the junkyard said, "there's a certified pre-owned champion out there waiting to be discovered. A car with guts, character, and the heart of a thoroughbred."

"And a body that won't run us more than five hundred bucks," Ray senior added.

Suddenly, a vintage horn blared through the junkyard. Maggie and her dad turned around, and Maggie saw it.

"He's perfect," she gasped.

Ray senior took one look at Herbie and smiled. "Just think," he said, patting the old car on the hood, "if that horn hadn't gone off, I never would have found—"

"This Mazda!" Maggie said, walking past Herbie again.

"I don't know, Maggie," Ray senior said, shaking his head. "Take a look at this guy. These puppies were built to last. They've got good engines, too. Just need to add the air bags."

"It's cute, but how much for the Mazda?" she asked the junkyard owner eagerly.

Ray senior walked to the Mazda and gave it a once-over as a giant magnet swooped down onto Herbie. It connected with Herbie's rear hood and hoisted him into the air. He frantically began beeping his horn, three short, three long. For a minute, Ray senior thought the car was sending out an SOS.

Maggie didn't notice. She was hoping to get a good price on the Mazda.

"I've had a lot of interest in this car," Dave said, "but since you're my first customer today, I might be able to cut you a deal."

He scrawled *199* in the dust on the Mazda's hood. Maggie pulled out the two hundred dollars that her father had given her. She was about to hand over the money when suddenly Herbie's rear hood broke away from the magnet. Maggie, Dave, and Ray senior jumped back as the car came crashing down, right on top of the Mazda.

Maggie looked at the crushed Mazda under the other car and sighed.

"I'll give you fifty for that one," she said glumly.

"Sorry. No can do," Dave said. "I always felt there was something special about this car. Something magical. I'd never sell it in a million years."

"Seventy-five," Maggie said flatly.

"Sold!" Dave said, snatching the money out of her hand.

"Well, at least we know the horn works," Ray senior said, giving his daughter a sly grin.

Chapter
6

Maggie fooled around on her skateboard as her dad filled Herbie's gas tank.

"Check it out," he said to Maggie. "The speedometer goes all the way to two hundred!"

"Well, somebody had a sense of humor," Maggie said, unimpressed.

"You're gassed up, tires are good, and the hood's back on," her dad said. "Bring it by the garage later; I'll have Augie look it over."

"Thanks, Dad," Maggie said. She got behind the wheel, ready to drive her new car home, when the glove box popped open. Maggie reached over to close it and noticed a dusty old letter inside. She tore the old envelope open and read the handwritten letter out loud:

"'Please take care of Herbie. Whatever your

problem, he'll help you find the answer.'"

"Great," Maggie said to herself, "a fortune cookie on wheels."

She turned the key to start the old engine. Suddenly, Herbie roared to life.

"Hey!" Maggie yelled as the car took off across the junkyard.

Maggie struggled to control the wheel as Herbie zigzagged through the yard. He finally skidded to a stop next to a shiny red sports car in a run-down barn.

Maggie jumped out of the car. She was a little spooked by the way he seemed to have a mind of his own. "I'm so sorry," she called to the mechanic working under the sports car. "I just got this junker and I think the gas pedal stuck. You okay?"

"Yeah," the mechanic answered, sliding out from under his car, "but it's the first time I've been involved in a hit-and-run in my own garage."

Maggie suddenly recognized the mechanic.

"Kevin?" she said in shock.

"Maggie? Wow!" he said, wiping the grease from his hands. "You look . . . *great.*"

The old friends hugged.

"Yeah," Maggie said, "wow . . . you too! What are you doing here?"

"Crazy Dave lets me work out of his place," Kevin explained. "I started my own custom car business. So what's up? I haven't seen you in like four years and suddenly you're trying to mow me down in an old junker."

"I'm just here for a few weeks to pack up and make a little cash before I head to New York."

Kevin smiled. "You've come a long way from the local go-kart championship."

Maggie rolled her eyes. "Well, the smell of hot wings still takes me back."

"We made a great team," Kevin said. "I remember you were going to be the first professional woman driver and I was going to be your crew chief. Crazy dreams, huh?"

"You're a great mechanic," Maggie said, tilting her head. "You could still totally make it."

"I don't know. Most drivers have the guys they came up through the ranks with in their pit crews. Anyway, I love doing this. Just me and the cars. Maybe one day I'll have Kevin's Custom Shops all over the state. For people like you," he said, looking at her new car, "with seriously impaired automotive taste."

Maggie laughed.

"He's just temporary wheels to get me from point A to B," she said, nodding at the rusted car.

The little car's engine rattled. That hurt his feelings.

Kevin walked around Herbie.

"The Maggie I knew wouldn't be caught dead in a car like this."

"That Maggie didn't have rent money to worry about."

Kevin thought for a moment. "What if I did the work for free?"

"This car is so not worth it," Maggie said. Herbie sagged on his wheels.

"I like the challenge," Kevin said, flipping a wrench in his hand.

"Okay, when do you want to start?"

"How about right now? Let's take him for a test drive."

Chapter 7

Maggie took a deep breath as she got behind the wheel. The engine turned over smoothly, and for the first time in years, Herbie made his way out of the junkyard.

He crawled down the street billowing white smoke from his tailpipe. Kevin concentrated on every wheeze and rattle the car made.

"We're not even doing the speed limit," Kevin complained to Maggie as every passing driver honked at the slow-moving car.

"If I go any faster the whole thing's gonna fall apart," she answered nervously.

"Let's head down to the fairgrounds," Kevin suggested. "They're having a car show. I tricked out this old sports car for the Hernandez brothers."

"I'm not really up for that whole scene anymore."

"Maggie, relax. You're looking at cars, not racing them."

"I doubt this bucket of bolts could make it down there anyway," Maggie said, disgusted. Suddenly, Herbie's engine revved, belching smoke! The little car tore across the intersection.

"Now, that's the Maggie I know!" Kevin shouted as Herbie popped up onto his two back tires.

"What are you talking about?" Maggie shouted back. "I'm not doing it! The pedal's stuck again!"

Maggie hit the brakes. Nothing happened. Panicked, she turned off the ignition and yanked out the key. Herbie screeched and skidded to a stop.

"He's got more horsepower than I expected," Kevin said, trying to catch his breath.

Maggie gasped, "I swear it wasn't me. It was Herbie."

Kevin raised his eyebrows and looked around. "Is Herbie here now?"

Maggie sighed. "The name came with the car."

Kevin took a deep breath. "Tell you what, let's take it back, strip it down, and get rid of all the old parts."

"Works for me," Maggie answered, turning the key. Herbie sputtered to life again. Maggie tried to take the car back to the junkyard, but it wouldn't turn right. "The steering column's jammed," Maggie said, confused.

"I guess we have to get back making all lefts," Kevin said.

But Herbie turned only when he wanted to.

"I'm being carjacked by my own car!" Maggie said, fighting the wheel.

Herbie finally pulled into a gated field. Maggie looked around. The field was covered with flashy neon-painted sports cars. "Oh no," Maggie said, cringing. The crowd of racers and their girlfriends laughed as Herbie cruised through the hot rods.

Suddenly, Herbie stalled. Maggie was in a panic. She turned the key, but Herbie's engine only whined. "Aw, man . . . ," she said, ducking down to the floor of the car.

Kevin seemed surprised.

"I thought you didn't want to come here," he said, perplexed.

"I didn't—it was Herbie!" Maggie insisted.

"Right," Kevin said, not believing her.

Maggie threw open the door and darted out.

She dashed into another row of cars and accidentally brushed against a gleaming hot rod. "Step away from the vehicle," the alarm blared in English, then in Japanese, *"Jidōsha O sawattenai de kudasai."*

The owner stopped the alarm when he saw Maggie. "Hey," he shouted, "look who decided to show!"

Maggie froze. There were Juan and Miguel Hernandez, the best street racers around.

"Hey, guys," she said, trying not to seem mortified. "What's up?"

Kevin got out of her car and walked over to Maggie and the Hernandez brothers. Miguel Hernandez looked over his sunglasses at Herbie, then at Maggie. "Is that your ride?" he asked her.

"No," Maggie said immediately, "I don't know whose it is."

Herbie heard what she said and sank down on his wheels.

Just then, an explosion of cheers rolled through the crowd. Every head turned toward the stage. Trip Murphy had arrived.

"You know him; you love and wanna be him," the announcer called out. "Let's hear it for a true champion, Riverside's own Trip Murphy!"

Trip took the microphone. "Hope you don't mind that I crashed your party."

The crowd went crazy. Trip raised his hand and tried to quiet them down. "When I'm in the middle of a race swapping paint with every other driver who wants my trophy, you know what keeps me going? It's you guys, my fans. Now I'm gonna give you that same experience in your own living room." Trip turned to his tattooed pit boss. "Crash, what's that on the backseat?"

Crash held up a plastic video game case and shrugged, pretending not to know what it was.

"Hey, it's my new video game, *Trip Murphy: Undefeated!* Is this even in stores yet?"

Crash shook his head.

"Then I guess this means you'll be the first to check it out," Trip said, grinning at the audience.

He tossed the game into the crowd; dozens of his fans jumped for it. Then he pulled back a sheet to reveal stacks of the game on a table. The people roared as two girls from Trip's team began to throw the games into the crowd. Trip waved as he left the stage.

"You've got a photo shoot in an hour," Crash said to him.

"No sweat. I'll just do two laps through the crowd. Keep the pens handy; I don't want to pit. And when the women give you their numbers, get photos this time. I don't want to replay what happened in Phoenix. I do enough charity work already," Trip ordered, laughing as he moved through the crowd and signed autographs.

"*Trip Murphy signed my head!*" somebody in the crowd screamed.

Maggie grabbed her skateboard out of the car.

"Where are you going?" Kevin asked.

"Anywhere but here."

"What about your car?"

"Tell Crazy Dave he can keep his money. I'll stick with my board."

Herbie began honking his horn frantically. Trip and the crowd turned to see where the commotion was coming from.

"What is wrong with this car?" Maggie said. "It's like it's trying to embarrass me on purpose."

She had popped the hood to kill the horn when a jet of oil squirted her in the face. Maggie looked down at her shirt. She was drenched.

She groaned as Trip and his ever-present camera crew headed her way.

Chapter
8

Trip continued signing autographs as he moved closer. Maggie was desperate. Kevin rummaged through the trunk of the car, looking for some rags to help her wipe the oil from her face.

Maggie turned to find Kevin holding up a racing helmet and a fire suit. "Some guy named Maxx left these in the trunk," Kevin said.

Maggie grabbed the fire suit and tossed the black helmet with MAXX airbrushed on its side into the car.

She zipped herself into the fire suit, then jumped into the driver's seat and said, "Let's go."

Maggie looked at the ignition. "Where are the keys?" she asked Kevin frantically. She spotted them on the floor of the car. As she reached down, Herbie's door slammed shut and gave her a push. Her head slid right into the helmet on the seat.

Suddenly, Trip Murphy was standing next to Herbie, looking at its helmeted driver. He reached in and signed the helmet.

Trip laughed. "I'd wear a helmet too if my ride looked like that," he said.

"Come on," Maggie said to Kevin as she turned the key. "Let's get out of here."

"Good idea, loser," Trip said to Kevin. "Better get that car back to the circus before the clowns put out an APB."

(53)

Herbie was steaming over Trip's insult as they chugged toward the gate of the fairgrounds.

"Look on the bright side," Kevin said. "You can sell the helmet on the Internet."

Maggie banged her head on the steering wheel. "Great, I can use the money to buy back what little dignity I have left."

Herbie spotted Trip's hot rod twenty feet away. Herbie started moving toward it. Maggie tried to turn the wheel, but she couldn't stop him.

Herbie stuck out his side mirror and scratched Trip's car from one end to the other.

"I swear I didn't do that," she hollered.

Kevin cringed as Trip rushed over to his car.

"Try explaining that to him," he said to Maggie.

"Race! Race! Race!" the crowd began to shout.

Trip nodded and gave a thumbs-up to the crowd.

"That thing?" he said to Crash as he got into his car. "What do I have to lose?"

Crash shrugged and joined the chanters. "Race! Race! Race!"

Maggie was in a panic. "I can't race!" she yelled at Kevin. "Get out there and tell him I'm sorry. I'll pay him back in installments."

Kevin jumped out of the car, but it was too late for Maggie. Herbie's door locks clicked and he moved toward the starting line.

"Kevin!" Maggie yelled. "Help! The car's kidnap—" But Herbie's windows rolled shut before she could finish.

Trip Murphy pulled up alongside her. "Don't worry; the pain will be gone in sixty seconds," he jeered.

Crash raised the starting flag. Trip flipped a switch, and the gauges on his dash came to life like the control panel on a 747.

Through the Maxx helmet, Maggie stared Trip in the eye. She pulled a knob on Herbie's dash and it came off in her hand. She groaned in disbelief and tried her best to put it back on.

"What are you trying to do to me, you crazy little car?"

Crash stepped between the two cars and threw down the green flag. Both cars burned rubber. The crowd was left coughing in a cloud of Herbie's smoke.

Trip's hot rod hit sixty miles per hour instantly. He laughed as he looked into his rearview. Nothing was there. Then he looked over, and Herbie was right alongside him!

Trip and Herbie were neck and neck. When Herbie's speedometer reached one hundred and ten miles per hour, Maggie couldn't believe it.

Herbie tried to pass, but Trip swerved, smashing into him. Herbie's hood flew open as he was knocked to the outside of the track. He spun out, doing two 360s, and ended up facing backward.

Herbie's hood snapped shut. His motor revved. Maggie floored it in reverse.

Trip was now doing one hundred and twenty five miles per hour. He looked over and couldn't believe what he saw. Herbie was right next to him, racing backward!

Trip swerved to smash into him again. Maggie screamed. This time Herbie braked, flipped up, and spun on his rear bumper. He landed facing forward, then rocketed ahead.

Trip was moving toward the finish line. Herbie was right on his tail. Trip released the nitrous into his engine for a burst of speed. He zoomed ahead.

Maggie shifted into fifth gear.

"Come on, Herbie," she cheered. Herbie swerved left and right, but he couldn't get around Trip. There were guardrails on both sides of the track.

Maggie took the wheel and turned it hard as she jumped the curb. Herbie landed on the guardrail. Sparks flew as he did a railslide past Trip. Maggie jumped him off the rail and over the finish line—a car's length ahead of Trip!

Kevin ran up to Herbie's window.

"Kevin, hop in!" Maggie yelled. "We're

getting out of here. If my dad finds out I raced, he's going to strap me to the underside of his car and run me five hundred laps."

The crowd was stunned into silence by Trip's defeat, then suddenly began to cheer for their new hero.

"You rock!" a fan called out to Maggie. "What's your name?"

Unsure, Maggie looked at Kevin.

"Maxx," Kevin yelled. "His name's Maxx. With two *x*'s. And he'll mop the road with Trip Murphy anytime, anywhere!"

Chapter 9

Inside Kevin's garage, Maggie took off the fire suit. "Did you see the way I came off the last turn and skipped onto the guardrail?" she said, still excited about the race.

Kevin shook his head. "I still don't know how you did that!"

"This is going to sound really strange," Maggie told him, "but it wasn't me. It was mostly Herbie."

Herbie's tires inflated with pride.

"News flash," Kevin said. "He's just a car."

"I can't explain it. When Trip was blocking me on the final turn, I kept wishing I was on my skateboard so I could railslide past him. Then Herbie kinda did it. I mean, it was like we were connected."

"Right," Kevin said, looking skeptical, "that makes total sense."

He kneeled down and took a look at the car's rusted tailpipe.

"What are you doing?" Maggie asked.

"Making sure the exhaust fumes aren't going back inside the car."

"Kevin, I beat the reigning champion in a '63 Love Bug named Herbie. How do you explain that?"

"You were in the zone," Kevin said, trying to be logical. "You had a great race. Why are you afraid to admit that to yourself?"

"Say what you want, but I'm telling you, there's something weird about this car."

"Well," Kevin said, rubbing some soot from the tailpipe between his fingers, "it was the sixties. Who knows what they put in the gas tank?"

Herbie swung his door into Kevin's stomach as he reached for the handle, knocking the wind out of him.

"Are you okay?" Maggie asked.

"Remind me to check the door springs," Kevin said, trying to catch his breath as he stood up straight.

Chapter 10

The next morning in the Peyton home, Maggie could hear her dad and her brother in the kitchen.

"It's a company that makes soap! What do they know about racing cars?" old man Peyton was saying as Maggie walked in.

"I guess enough to get off a sinking ship," her brother responded dryly.

"Did another sponsor bite the dust?" Maggie asked them.

"They come and they go." Ray senior shrugged. "It's part of the business."

He raised an eyebrow at Maggie. "You got in kinda late last night."

Maggie looked at her dad. "Let me direct you to the birth date on my driver's license," she said.

Her dad smiled. "You'll never be so old that I stop worrying about you, spark plug."

Sally from Bass Pro appeared at the kitchen door.

"Don't tell me you're pulling out too," old man Peyton asked her.

"No," Sally said, coming through the door and turning on the Peytons' TV set. "I'm making your day."

Sally and the Peyton family saw the words "Trip Murphy: Invincible?" on the screen.

They looked at one another in shock. Maggie's jaw dropped as the announcer said, "Taking the sports world by storm, here it is again, our exclusive footage of Trip Murphy getting scorched in an impromptu street race. Get this: the competition was a 1963 Volkswagen Beetle. That's right, folks, a '63 Love Bug!"

Old man Peyton walked out into the driveway. Maggie followed right behind him. "I'm sensing you're looking for an explanation," she said to her dad as he walked around the old car.

"You promised no more street racing," he said, upset. "I almost lost you once. I'm not going to stand by and let you do it again."

"Can the defendant get a word in?" Maggie pleaded.

"Take the stand," her dad said. "I'm all ears."

Maggie shuffled her feet. "I kinda ran into Kevin yesterday."

"Kevin? Figures. You're home less than twenty-four hours and he's already got you street racing again. Maggie, I didn't work my butt off putting you through school so you could end up back behind the wheel of a race car."

"I wasn't driving, okay?" Maggie said, flustered. "It was his friend . . . um . . . Maxx. They wanted to challenge Trip. So I let them borrow my car. It was a one-shot deal."

Maggie couldn't believe she had just lied to her dad, but she knew he'd never forgive her for racing again. And she knew for sure he wouldn't believe that the car had made her do it!

"Tell you one thing," Ray senior said, looking at the car. "That Maxx guy must be one heck of a racer to beat Trip Murphy."

(53)

Chapter

II

Trip Murphy was holding up a bottle of aftershave.

"Life's a trip; then you drive," he said, giving the camera his best stony-eyed stare. He was filming one of his many commercial endorsements.

The director tried to smile. "Cut! Okay, let's print take thirty-two and move on to the next setup."

Trip signed some autographs for the crew as he walked toward his manager, Larry. Larry was also his brother.

"Trip, I need five minutes. I've got sponsors chewing up my backside." Larry pointed at three executives standing in front of Trip's tour bus. Not one of them looked happy.

Larry looked at the TV crew huddled by the

fence. "And a television special going down the drain because you banished the film crew to Siberia."

Trip wanted no part of the crew. "I don't want to talk about yesterday."

"We're not talking about yesterday. We're talking about tomorrow and the next day. This is your future, Trip, and these are the people paying for it. Get your head back in the game."

"I can't deal with this right now," Trip said, rushing into his tour bus to avoid the press and the executives.

He hit a button on his TV remote and watched the race from the day before again.

"It doesn't make any sense," he said, watching Herbie on tape. "How could that thing beat me?"

"Nobody cares about some stupid street race," Larry said.

"I care! I'm a champion who just got beat," Trip growled. "I've been up all night going over that race. I outclassed him on every front."

"Trip, it's me. Your brother. The guy who taught you how to drive. I'm telling you to forget about it. Look, those sports reporters will get a few laughs; by

Thursday they won't even remember it happened."

"I want a rematch," Trip said, staring at Herbie barreling across the finish line. "I'm thinking of a two-day racing event. I beat all comers, then trounce this one."

"This is insane on so many levels," Larry told him. "How do you even know this Maxx guy will show up?"

"I want posters in every garage, body shop, and auto parts store in the area and full-page ads in all the local rags. Maxx is a racer. He'll show."

"Great, and who is going to pay for all this?"

"That's *your* problem, Larry. Talk to the sponsors," Trip snapped angrily.

"Mr. Murphy, they need you back on set," said a production assistant on the other side of the trailer door.

"Be right there," Trip answered.

"Trip," Larry pleaded, "please don't do this."

"Larry, I'm going to exterminate that car."

(53)

Chapter
12

A full-page ad in the newspaper the next day laid out the challenge:

THINK YOU CAN BEAT TRIP MURPHY? THEN BRING IT ON! TWO-DAY ELIMINATION EVENT. $10,000 GRAND PRIZE!

The newspaper was lying on the floor of Kevin's garage, but he and Maggie had not seen the ad. They were too busy looking at plans to overhaul Herbie.

"I figure we can turn him into a serious champion," Kevin told Maggie. "There are a couple of races coming up and I—"

"Whoa," Maggie said, cutting him off. "The other day was great. I still don't know how it happened, but it was a fluke, never to be repeated."

"But you said you loved being back behind the

wheel," Kevin argued, knowing Maggie was a born race driver.

"I did," Maggie said, trying to explain. "In that swan-song, farewell-tour kinda way. Besides, I'm moving to New York and starting my new life."

"C'mon, Mags," Kevin pleaded. "No way can you move to a city where you take the subway to work."

"I promised my dad no more street racing, then I ended up lying to his face. The last time I did that, I wound up in the hospital for two weeks. Please note the vicious after-school-special cycle I'm trying to break. I just need to make some quick cash to pay for my apartment."

Kevin picked up the newspaper and tossed it at her. "Well, here are the classifieds. Better get cracking."

As the newspaper fell, it opened to Trip's racing ad. Herbie silently rolled forward. His headlights eagerly scanned the ad.

"Look, I'm sorry," Maggie said, picking up the paper but still not noticing the ad. "I worked really hard to get this TV gig."

Kevin shrugged. "What are you going to

do about your car when you leave?"

"I'll drop off the keys and get the number of a good exorcist," she said, smirking.

Herbie watched Maggie, hoping she would see the ad in the newspaper. But Maggie tossed the paper toward the trash and got into Herbie's front seat.

Suddenly, Herbie's hood began to open and close frantically. Maggie clutched the wheel as Herbie created a gust of wind that blew the newspaper out of the trash can. It fluttered in the air and landed on the windshield. Trip Murphy's ad was now spread right in front of her face.

Kevin ran to the driver's side as Herbie's windshield wipers came to life and slapped the ad into his hands.

Kevin and Maggie looked at the ad offering a ten-thousand-dollar prize.

"I know what you're thinking, Maggie, but it's just one race," Kevin said excitedly. "Let's get practical. Ten grand's a lot of cash. We could split it. You'll have enough for rent money and I'll have enough to fix up this dump. Everybody wins."

Kevin held up her helmet and smiled.

"What do you say . . . Maxx?"

Chapter
13

The next day, Kevin and Maggie faced an arsenal of gleaming new parts for Herbie. They spent the day installing everything from new tires and a spoiler to a nitrous tank and an oxygen sensor.

Kevin swapped out the round steering wheel for a cool batwing racing wheel. He took Herbie to a car wash for a much-needed bath. The little car was looking better and better.

After a few test laps, Kevin drove Herbie back to the garage to make a few final adjustments.

"Let's push back on the seat," he said to Maggie as they tried to check the steering column. "One, two—"

Suddenly, the seats lurched forward, pushing Maggie and Kevin nose to nose. They struggled to wiggle out of the car, but only managed to push their faces closer together. For a moment, Kevin thought that he and Maggie were going to kiss, but Maggie just laughed until Herbie's seats finally popped back.

Kevin climbed out of the car, a little embarrassed. He took a long look at the headlights and bumper, which seemed to be smiling at him, and shook his head.

(53)

Meanwhile, at Trip Murphy's gleaming, high-tech garage, Trip and Crash were studying a 3-D computerized model of Herbie.

"I've been over every inch of this model ten times," Crash said. "I've run all the tests. There's no way an ordinary engine like that could have smoked yours."

Trip stared at the car with pure hatred. "There's nothing ordinary about that car," he said. "I don't know what's under its hood, but I'm going to find out."

Chapter 14

That evening, Maggie and Kevin took Herbie out for another test drive. "Uh-oh," Maggie said as Herbie turned into the lot of an old drive-in movie. "Herbie's gone autopilot on me again!"

It was the same drive-in Kevin where and Maggie had gone on their one and only date. Kevin smiled at Maggie; he still did not believe that Herbie had a mind of his own.

"Very funny, Mags," he said, looking around. "What are we doing here?"

"I don't know," Maggie said. "Ask Herbie."

She began laughing as she remembered the disastrous date. "How did I know the police were going to come after us?"

Kevin laughed too.

"That usually happens when you hotwire your dad's car and take it without permission. I was this close to kissing you when the deputies surrounded us."

"Maybe it was fate's way of saying we should just be friends," Maggie said. "Okay, trip down memory lane over."

She tried to turn Herbie around when the little car lurched up to the ticket gate. Before Kevin and Maggie knew it, they were parked in front of the giant screen. A romantic black-and-white tearjerker was playing.

Herbie watched the screen too and soon began leaking tears of oil from his grill. The whole car shuddered as Herbie cried.

"Did you feel that?" Kevin asked Maggie.

"It's Herbie," Maggie sighed. "He's kind of emotional."

Kevin couldn't figure out why he was sitting in a car watching a love story with a girl who was supposed to be just a friend.

"Okay, Mags," he finally asked, "are you hitting on me?"

Just then the song "Reunited" began playing on the radio. "I'm telling you, Herbie's doing this! Bad car. Bad car!" Maggie said, scolding Herbie.

Kevin shook his head. "Look, you're moving to

New York and I'm staying here. Long-distance relationships never work. I mean, it's not like we stayed in touch when you were at college."

"Don't pin that on me," Maggie told him. "You could have totally come down and hung out."

Kevin shrugged. "Figured you wanted your space. Didn't need your gearhead friend hanging around, reminding you that you wrapped your car around a tree."

"I never blamed you, Kevin. The fact is, I lost my nerve and I was afraid to get back behind the wheel. I didn't want you to be disappointed in me."

"That wouldn't have happened," Kevin said when a loud honk came from the car. Herbie was blowing his nose.

"It's been a long day," Kevin said, still confused. "We should get going."

Herbie finally obeyed as Maggie started the engine and headed out of the drive-in. "How about I buy you dinner?" she said.

"Better make it quick. Wouldn't want your magic car turning into a pumpkin before we get home."

Chapter 15

"I'll have a rib sandwich and some slaw," Kevin said at the counter of his favorite restaurant, the BBQ Coach. Maggie looked around as Kevin ordered, and suddenly she gasped.

"Oh, I don't believe this," she said in a low voice to Kevin. "We can't stay here."

Kevin rolled his eyes. "Don't tell me you've gone vegan."

"No," Maggie whispered, "it's my brother—on drums."

Kevin looked at the rock band playing at the far end of the restaurant.

"Come on," Maggie said, pulling his arm. "Let's go!" But it was too late. The band was taking a break, and Maggie's brother spotted her.

"What are you doing here?" Ray asked, surprised to see her.

"What am I doing here?" Maggie answered nervously. "I'm having some curly fries. What are you doing here? If Dad finds out about this, he's going to have a coronary! You've got a huge race in less than a week. Is playing with Stu and the guys more important than your career?"

Ray shuffled his feet as he thought it over.

"Well, I bet Dad would be interested to know you and Kevin are going out again."

Maggie overreacted.

"We're not going out! We were never going out. We're just friends."

"Just friends . . . ," Kevin agreed with a smile.

Ray nodded.

"I won't tell if you won't tell," her brother said. He spit in his hand and offered it to her. "Spit swear!"

"This is so gross," Maggie said as she spit in her own hand and shook on it. "We never saw each other tonight."

Ray grinned at his sister and gave Kevin a friendly slap on the back. Then he headed back to the stage for the band's next set.

"Great, now I have to keep *his* secret too," Maggie groaned.

"They're pretty good," Kevin said, watching the band for a moment. He turned back to Maggie. "Look. Ray's doing what he loves. And you're doing what you love. Why don't you both be out and proud about the whole thing?"

Maggie shook her head. She knew that Kevin just didn't understand.

53

As Maggie walked into the Peyton house that night, she heard her dad talking to Sally from Bass Pro. "You can't let them drop us, Sally. You're all we got. It would break Ray junior's heart."

Maggie listened.

"No," Sally said to Ray senior, "it would break *your* heart. When are you going to open your eyes? Ray's not cut out for racing. I've held out as long as I can, but I can't do this anymore. Bass Pro's dropping you. I'm sorry."

Sally stood up and walked toward the door.

"Sal, wait," Ray senior said, following her tentatively. "Ask them to hold on until the California race. If Ray doesn't place, I'll close up shop and go sell motor oil or something."

"I'll do my best, but you're going to have to

plead your case directly. The boys in the front office are coming out this week. I'll set up a meeting."

Maggie heard the screen door slam as Sally left. Ray senior walked into the kitchen and saw his daughter at the table. "How long have you been sitting here?"

"Long enough," Maggie answered, looking up at her dad's tired face.

He patted her on the shoulder. "I'm so glad you're out of this, spark plug. At least I did one thing right."

Old man Peyton headed up the stairs as Maggie sat in the darkened kitchen and thought about Trip's ten-thousand-dollar challenge.

Chapter 16

The next day, Maggie and Kevin were towing Herbie to the track. Maggie stared out the window as they zoomed through the desert. "Now's about the time you're supposed to talk me out of this," she said nervously.

"No can do," Kevin said as they pulled into a massive parking area. It was filled with hundreds of the coolest cars in the world. Herbie was scoping out the competition from under his tarp. Everyone there wanted a chance to beat Trip and take that ten-thousand-dollar prize.

"These guys are really serious, Kevin."

"And so are you," Kevin said, trying to reassure her.

While Kevin began unhitching Herbie, Maggie stepped up to the sign-in booth. She turned and

Maggie is the first Peyton to graduate from college.

Maggie looks for the right car.

Herbie has a mind of his own.

Kevin gets to work on Herbie.

Herbie before . . .

. . . and Herbie after!

Ray Junior is a great brother but a lousy driver.

Trip Murphy is a great driver but a lousy guy.

Maggie makes a very bad decision . . .

. . . and Herbie pays for it.

Maggie and Herbie become an unbeatable team.

Maggie was born to drive.

Maggie and Herbie win the big race!

Trip loses the race . . . and his mind.

Kevin kisses a racing champion!

saw Trip and Crash. "Who are you signing up?" Trip asked her. "In the Way Ray?"

"Actually, I'm sponsoring Maxx," Maggie told them. She nodded at Kevin, who whipped off the tarp, unveiling the new street-racing Herbie. The little car gleamed in the California sun. He had a double exhaust, neon purple running lights, and a huge engine. Trip blinked. Herbie's spinning chrome rims were almost blinding.

The crowd looked on, impressed. "What do you think of the makeover?" Maggie asked Trip.

Trip sneered. "You can take the car out of the junkyard, but you can't take the junkyard out of the car. How do you know this Maxx guy, anyway?"

"Um . . . we go way back," Maggie said coyly.

Trip nodded. "I want to meet him. Can you arrange a face-to-face?"

"He's, uh . . . meditating," Maggie answered. "Getting into the zone."

"Pressure getting to him?"

Maggie smiled. "I don't think he's too worried. He's already beaten you once."

"Beginner's luck," Trip said confidently. "Tell Maxx I'm looking forward to the rematch."

Maggie took a breath as Trip and Crash walked away. "I don't know if I can do this," she said to Kevin.

Kevin wasn't nervous. He patted her on the back. "It's just prerace jitters. That's all."

"More like prerace nervous breakdown," Maggie answered as she reached for the black fire suit and helmet.

Chapter 17

Kevin and Maxx looked at the elimination board. The winners of each round would go on to the next race until all but one racer were eliminated. "You're in the first race," Kevin said to her.

Trip Murphy stepped up to the elimination board. "There are two hundred names up there," he shouted to the crowd. "By the end of the day, there'll only be one left. That driver will face me tomorrow and have the chance to win this. . . ."

He held up a supersized check for ten thousand dollars.

"Whose name is going to be on this check? Will it be yours?" Trip said, pointing at one of the drivers. "Yours?" he shouted, whipping up the crowd. "Or yours?" he said, pointing at Maxx.

"There's only one way to find out. *Let's race!*"

In her black fire suit and helmet, Maggie pulled Herbie up to the starting line. He bounced excitedly on his new hydraulics, tilting forward and back.

Herbie jumped back into starting position just as the air horn blasted. The race was on.

Herbie took off like a bullet. Maggie's helmet pressed against the headrest as Herbie shot ahead of the pack.

On the track, the Hernandez brothers were trying to catch up with Herbie. They both fired their nitrous tanks and rocketed ahead of the fast little race car. The brothers tried to close in to block Herbie from moving forward. But Herbie blasted through them to cross the finish line first as if they were standing still. The day's first race was his!

"Whoa," yelled Maggie as the crowd went wild. Herbie honked his horn gleefully in response.

Herbie won again and again that day until every car was eliminated. They would be racing Trip Murphy the next day for the ten grand.

Trip watched from the top of his tour bus. He couldn't believe it. The crowd had been won over by Maxx's car!

Later, Trip sat with his laptop, examining photos of the races. He zoomed in on a photo of the helmeted Maxx. He zoomed in more and more until a strand of familiar red hair appeared on the screen. Trip was stunned. He leaned back into his plush tour bus sofa and smiled.

"Gotcha, Maxx!"

Chapter
18

That night in the desert, a party was in full swing. Maggie exchanged her fire suit for a black dress.

"Wow," Kevin said when he saw her. "You clean up great for someone who changed in a portable toilet."

Maggie rolled her eyes. "I'm sure there's a compliment in there somewhere."

As they walked toward the party, Kevin noticed that Herbie was bumper to bumper with a cute little yellow sports car. Herbie's headlights burned at a low smolder.

"Hey, how did Herbie get over here?" he asked, looking at the empty spot where he had parked Herbie earlier. Kevin shook his head. "I think I'm officially losing my mind."

"That was my first reaction," Maggie said,

laughing, "but then I embraced the mystery that is Herbie."

She leaned over to Herbie and nodded toward the pretty yellow sports car.

"She's too young for you," Maggie teased. Herbie's wheels deflated a little.

Walking in the moonlight, Kevin thought that Maggie had never looked more beautiful.

"Winning definitely suits you," he told her. He reached into his pocket and pulled out a small box. "I got you something."

Maggie opened the box and took out a silver necklace. "It's amazing!" she said, holding up the silver chain in the moonlight. A silver circle with Herbie's number fifty-three dangled from the chain.

"It's for luck tomorrow," Kevin said bashfully. Then the moment finally seemed right to both of them. Kevin and Maggie leaned toward each other to kiss.

Suddenly, the couple was hit by two blinding high beams. Maggie and Kevin shielded their eyes. Trip Murphy was stepping out from the headlights.

"Trip," Maggie said, "I hardly recognize you without your camera crew."

Trip smirked. "I gave them the night off. Can we talk?" he said to Maggie, then nodded at Kevin. "Alone."

"It's cool," Kevin said, not really wanting to let Maggie walk off with Trip. "I've already got his autograph."

Maggie and Trip walked a short distance away.

"Your driver, Maxx, did pretty well today, for an amateur. But he's got some serious flaws. Take his car, for instance. For one, this car's chassis's too high; aerodynamics are all wrong."

"Thanks for the tip." Maggie shrugged. "I'll pass it along to Maxx."

"You know what I can't figure out?" Trip said as they walked along. "Why you're not behind the wheel. I hear you were a heck of a street racer back in the day."

"Ancient history," Maggie answered.

"I doubt that. It's in your blood. Your grandfather was one of the greatest drivers to ever hit the track. I remember watching him as a kid beat Cale Yarborough with a cracked engine block."

"Wow," Maggie said, surprised. "You know your history."

"The man was my hero. He was the reason I got into racing. I've got to believe it's hotwired into your DNA. Heck, your dad ought to get Ray out of number eighty-six and give you a shot."

"How many women drivers have ever won a major championship?" she said to him seriously.

"It only takes one person to blaze a trail. Ever think you're the next great Peyton? Want to see how it feels behind the wheels of a real car?"

Trip nodded toward his amazing stock car. Suddenly, Maggie was really listening.

"You serious?" she asked.

"Go on," Trip said, handing her the keys. "It'll be our little secret.

"Try to keep it under three hundred!" Trip laughed as Maggie got behind the wheel.

The car felt incredible in her hands. Maggie hit the gas. "WHOOOOOOOOOOOOOOOOOOA!" she yelled as the powerful stock car roared into the desert.

(53)

Trip knew that a driver like Maggie would be enjoying herself for a while. He made sure the coast was clear, then walked over to Herbie. "Okay," he said as he popped Herbie's hood, "let's see what makes you tick."

Trip leaned in and laughed. "There's no way you could beat me with this engine."

Herbie dropped his hood on Trip's head. "*Ahhhhh!*" Trip yelled.

A jet of oil squirted into Trip's face as he tried to pull himself free.

"You want a piece of me?" he shouted at Herbie, finally prying the hood open. He grabbed a wrench and brought it down on Herbie's engine. "Who's laughing now? Huh?" he said as he swung the wrench again.

Herbie popped his hood again and caught Trip under the chin. The force knocked Trip into the dirt.

Trip stood up slowly and rubbed his jaw. "It's only a car," he said to himself as Herbie's headlights flashed on and off in his face.

Out of the desert, doing two hundred miles per hour, Maggie suddenly turned and roared toward Trip and Herbie.

"That was unbelievable!" she said as she pulled to a stop. "I've never driven anything like it. That was the most awesome driving experience of my life."

Herbie did *not* like the sound of that.

"It's amazing what a real car can do, isn't it?" Trip said, giving Herbie a dirty look. "Someday maybe you'll have one of your own."

Maggie sighed as she stepped out of the stock car. "Yeah, in my dreams."

"Maybe not," Trip said, putting his arm around her. "I've got a little proposition for you. How about we make tomorrow's race for pinks, too?"

"I don't know," Maggie said. "Herbie's pretty special."

"Get real," Trip said with an evil grin. "Nobody's going to take you seriously in that thing. But you drive home in Trip Murphy's stock car, your dad would be an idiot not to put you on the team."

Maggie thought about what it would be like to race as the next great Peyton. "What do you say?" Trip asked, smiling.

Maggie threw out her hand and shook on it.

Chapter 19

The next morning, Maggie dashed to the kitchen. That day was going to be the race of her life, and she was already running late.

"Ray," she called to her brother as she ran toward the open refrigerator, "if you've drunk all the orange juice, I'm going to kill you."

The fridge door swung shut, and there stood Maggie's best friend. "Charisma!" Maggie yelled.

"Mag-Wheels!" Charisma squealed. She leaned in and gave Maggie a big hug. "The two Rays told me to make myself at home. They were running out to some sponsor thingy. I didn't really understand; I just nodded and smiled. I've had a lot of practice in Paris."

Maggie was stunned. "Why aren't you still in France?"

"Paris was a drag," Charisma said, shrugging as if

flying thousands of miles on a whim was no big deal.

Charisma bit into a piece of toast.

"So I figured I'd come back and we'd start our road trip early," she said, smiling.

"Um . . . slight problem," Maggie said, looking at the time. "I promised I'd meet a friend out in the desert."

"Why?" Charisma asked, looking around. "Are you going to bury a body?"

"Actually, he's racing in a tournament."

Charisma nodded. "You think you're pretty clever, but I can see right through you, Mags."

"You can?" Maggie asked nervously.

Charisma gave her a wink. "It's obvious. You're dating him."

"Okay, if you say so," Maggie answered, relieved.

"Don't be coy. What's his name? Is it serious?"

"Uh, Maxx," Maggie told her, "and we're so close, we're practically the same person."

Maggie and Charisma drove out to the desert track. Almost every person in the crowd was wearing a Maxx T-shirt. Charisma was shocked.

"How popular is your boyfriend?" she asked Maggie.

Maggie just smiled.

Charisma suddenly started waving. "Hey, look, there's your dad," she said, spotting Sally and Ray senior. "Mr. P.!" she shouted. "We're over—"

Maggie put her hand over Charisma's mouth. As she did an about-face with Charisma on her arm, she suddenly came face to face with Ray junior. Maggie desperately tried to seem casual.

"Aren't you supposed to be at some sponsor event?" she asked her brother, wishing he was.

"This is it, genius," Ray junior said, gesturing to the track. "Sally dragged us out here to glad-hand some of the Bass Pro execs. I thought you'd be home packing for your road trip."

"We had to come and support Maggie's boyfriend," Charisma said brightly.

"Kevin?" Ray junior asked.

"No, Maxx!" Charisma squealed. "Who's Kevin? Aren't you dating Maxx?"

"No—yes!" Maggie blurted out.

Ray junior shook his head. "That's cold. Kevin's so obviously into you, and then this guy Maxx comes out of nowhere—I can't believe you go for that macho thing. I mean, what's with the helmet?"

"Dad's going to wonder where you are," Maggie said to her brother impatiently.

Ray shrugged and turned to walk off. "You tell Maxx I want to meet him. Nobody dates my sister without my say-so."

Charisma was shocked. "I go to Paris to find romance and you're juggling two hotties in Riverside? That's it; I'm never leaving the country again."

Maggie's walkie-talkie beeped. It was Kevin. "Mags, we've got a little situation going on with Herbie."

"I'll be there in ten seconds," Maggie answered.

Charisma stomped her foot. "Herbie? Don't tell me; you've got three guys on the hook?"

"Just wait here," Maggie said as she dashed off.

"Where have you been?" Kevin asked her when she showed up out of breath.

"In a nightmare," Maggie huffed, "where my dad, brother, and best friend from college all decided to show up."

Kevin pointed to Herbie. "We've got another

problem. Herbie's freaking out. I've gone over everything twice. I can't find anything wrong. He's just not firing on all cylinders. You didn't leave him alone with Trip last night, did you?"

But before Maggie could explain, Charisma walked up, and the five-minute warning to race time sounded. Maggie was about to burst from the pressure.

"Who's that?" Kevin asked as he looked at Charisma.

"Your new problem," Maggie sighed. "I need you to keep her away from my dad. Oh yeah, and she thinks I'm dating Maxx. Don't ask me to explain."

Kevin was too confused to ask.

"Get suited up," he said, "and have a heart-to-heart with your car."

"Herbie," Maggie pleaded, "what's going on? I don't have time for this right now. We need to get out there and beat Trip. Just get a grip. You're a car. Do what I tell you to do! Okay?"

Maggie grabbed her gym bag from Herbie's trunk and left to change. As she walked away, steam hissed from Herbie's engine.

53

Chapter
20

Kevin and Charisma waited for the race to start. "Where's Maggie?" Charisma asked, looking around for her friend.

"Um . . . with Maxx," Kevin answered. "He was pretty nervous."

Charisma looked at Kevin. "It must be hard for you, seeing them together."

Kevin tried not to laugh. "I don't think it will last," he said. "Maxx isn't really her type."

Charisma nodded sympathetically.

"You keep telling yourself that," she said. Then she added with a mischievous twinkle in her eye, "And just remember: there are other cars in the lot."

"Good to know," Kevin was saying when the announcer's voice came over the PA system.

"It's a beautiful day for a race. Trip Murphy's been cooling his heels in the wings, waiting for his challenger to come out first, but so far, nothing—hold on, looks like Trip's had enough waiting."

Trip made his grand entrance onto the track, his car engine roaring.

As Trip's car rolled to the starting line, little Herbie chugged into view.

"Is that . . . ? Yes, it is!" the announcer said. "Number fifty-three has decided to show."

"Blow his wheels off, Maggie!" Kevin yelled.

Charisma shot him a look.

"I mean Maxx," Kevin said quickly. "That's what I call him. It's, uh, my little nickname for him."

Up in the stands, Ray senior was shocked. "Isn't that Maggie's car?" he asked Sally and Ray junior.

The crowd became silent as the green starting flag went up. In an instant the flag dropped. Trip and Maggie disappeared down the track in a cloud of dust.

Tearing across the desert, the two cars were neck and neck. Maggie looked at her speedometer—110—120! She could feel her heart pounding. She looked over at Trip. He smiled as he floored the gas, leaving Maggie and Herbie far behind.

"He's pulling ahead!" Maggie said out loud, admiring Trip's dazzling machine. "Look at the way that car handles!"

Herbie didn't like the remark and narrowed his eyes. Maggie pushed the gas pedal to the floor. The little car zoomed ahead, passing Trip and racing toward the finish line.

Maggie waved at Trip as the crowd cheered. Then suddenly Herbie slowed down. The finish line was just a few feet ahead. "What are you doing!" Maggie screamed. "Come on!"

Herbie braked and skidded off into the desert as Trip crossed the finish line.

Furious, Maggie climbed out of the car. "You stupid car!" she yelled. "You blew that on purpose. I thought you were supposed to help me!"

Trip walked over. "Your voice is a little more high pitched than I expected," he said to her. "But it sounds familiar. Come on, Maxx, take off the helmet and show us who you really are."

Maggie reached up and pulled off her helmet.

The crowd gasped. "It's a chick!" Miguel Hernandez yelled.

"That ain't no chick," his brother Juan yelled. "It's Maggie!"

Trip grinned.

"Guess I was wrong about you. You're not the next great Peyton after all," he said cruelly. "You're just another amateur who choked in the clutch."

Kevin fought his way through the crowd.

"Maggie!" he shouted as he tried to reach her, but Maggie was storming away.

"Look, you had a bad day," he said, grabbing her arm. "Let's get out of here and take Herbie back to the garage. There's always another race."

"No, there's not. It's over. I should never have done this in the first place."

Kevin saw Crash attaching Herbie to a tow truck. Kevin yelled, "Hey, get away from him!"

"Maggie didn't tell you?" Trip said, gloating. "We were racing for pinks. It was a little deal we made last night after I let her race my car. Said it was the best ride of her life."

"Please tell me you really didn't do that," Kevin said to Maggie in disbelief.

"I'm so sorry, Kevin."

"Don't apologize to me," Kevin said, walking away. "Apologize to Herbie. He's the one you stabbed in the back."

Maggie stared at the sad little car. Trip shrugged and gave her a look that said *You can't win them all*.

Then, looking at Herbie, he said, "Payback time."

53

Ray senior walked up as they towed Herbie away.

"How could you lie to me, Maggie?" he asked her in disbelief and disappointment.

Maggie bowed her head. "I can explain."

Ray senior frowned at his daughter.

"I'm through listening, Maggie. There used to be a time when your word meant something. I thought your old man taught you the value of honesty. Guess he didn't."

"Daddy, wait," Maggie said, but Ray senior walked away, sadly shaking his head.

Chapter
21

The next day, Maggie sat slumped in the passenger seat of Charisma's hybrid. She stared blankly out the window.

"I still can't believe you were pulling a racer X on everybody," Charisma said.

"I thought we agreed to have a nice, conversation-free ride," Maggie replied, still depressed.

"We've been friends for four years and I never knew the real you until today."

"Yeah." Maggie nodded. "A lying backstabber who managed to alienate everyone she cares about."

"You don't get it, do you?" Charisma said excitedly. "You were awesome out there. Why are you going to New York? You belong behind the wheel of a race car!"

Maggie shrugged. "I have a career path that I'm very excited about."

"And Albert Einstein was all set up to work in the patent office, but that's not where he belonged. Are you really going to be happy reporting on the story, rather than being one yourself?"

As Charisma drove, Maggie spotted the twisted tree she'd hit long ago. "Stop the car!" she said, startling Charisma.

Maggie stepped out and placed her hand on the tree. Charisma was right behind her.

"Why are we touching that tree?" she asked Maggie.

"It's the reason I gave up my dream," Maggie said, suddenly feeling stronger. "I'm not going to make the same mistake twice. We're turning around," she told Charisma. "And I'm driving."

"Why?" Charisma asked as Maggie got behind the wheel and floored it.

"Because if you drove any slower, you'd be Amish!" Maggie said, speeding to Trip's garage.

"I'm still confused about the whole tree thing," Charisma said, trying to hold on.

The hybrid screeched up to Trip's garage. Maggie hopped out and ran inside.

"Trip, we need to talk," she said.

Trip looked at her smugly.

"Amateur hour is over," he said mockingly. "I've got a *real* race to prepare for."

"I want to buy Herbie back," she said, biting her lip.

"Herbie?" Trip said, looking around.

"My car," Maggie said, clarifying what she meant.

"Oh, that," Trip said, grinning. "I'd really love to help, but you're too late. Crash just took him out for a little spin."

Maggie felt a wave of panic go through her. "Where is he, Trip?"

Chapter
22

Maggie raced into Jimmy D.'s Crash and Bash Demolition Derby, hoping that she was not too late. Herbie was in the middle of the mud-filled arena. The little car had been stripped of all his extras. He was just plain old Herbie again.

She watched as Crash walked toward Herbie. He pulled out a can of spray paint and drew big bull's-eyes on Herbie's sides. The crowd cheered, and Crash jumped into the driver's seat.

Nine monster demolition cars surrounded Herbie. The driver of a huge monster truck with eight-foot wheels stuck his head out and pointed at Herbie. "Ten cars enter, one car leaves!" he screamed.

The crowd in the stands joined in the chanting. *"Ten cars enter, one car leaves! Ten cars enter, one car leaves!"*

Herbie looked so helpless in the middle of the ring. Suddenly, an air horn blasted, and the demolition car drivers hit the gas. All of them aimed for Herbie.

Maggie tried to jump the railing, but a security guard stopped her. "Sorry. Drivers only," he said, holding her back.

"You don't understand, that's my car!"

"Well, you parked it in the wrong spot," the owner of the derby said as he walked up to Maggie. "Name's Jimmy D. This is my place and that car belongs to me."

"How much to buy him back?" Maggie asked desperately.

Jimmy D. looked into Maggie's eyes and saw something he hadn't seen in a long time: someone who had a real love for her car.

"Tell you what," he said with a small smile, "if it makes it out of here in one piece, I'll give it back to you for free."

Maggie looked back at the ring just as an old pickup broadsided her car. She put her hand over her eyes and heard the horrible sound of Herbie's body being crushed.

When the truck backed up, Maggie saw Herbie's

fender fall, and his lights began to dim.

Suddenly, four cars revved their engines and charged toward him from four directions.

"Herbie, don't give up," Maggie yelled as she hopped over the concrete divider.

"Hey!" the security guard yelled. The huge monster truck, which had a battered old cowcatcher welded to its front, was about to ram Herbie.

"Go, Maggie. Go!" Charisma shouted from the stands.

"Herbie, fight back!" Maggie shouted as she ran toward him. "I can't lose you! We're a team!"

The demolition cars zoomed past Maggie.

"I need you, Herbie!" Maggie cried. Herbie heard her, and a spark glowed in his heart.

Inside Herbie, Crash was completely confused. Herbie's back wheels began to spin. His motor roared!

The monster truck shot forward, and Herbie flipped onto his back. His sunroof dropped over Maggie, protecting her from the huge truck.

Maggie and Crash held on inside Herbie as he flipped back onto his wheels.

"I didn't do that," Crash screamed. "It was the car!"

"His name is Herbie," Maggie yelled.

Herbie's driver's-side door sprang open, and Maggie kicked Crash out. She took the wheel. "Let's get outta here," she said to Herbie as Crash ran out of the arena.

Maggie headed Herbie for the arena exit, but two cars cut them off.

Herbie tipped up on his left wheels as one car charged him like a bull.

"Olé!" the crowd yelled as the car passed under Herbie's raised wheels. Herbie tipped up on his right side. His tires bounced across the roof of the next charging car. Both cars smashed into the arena wall as the crowd screamed.

The only cars left standing were Herbie and the monster truck. It roared its engine and headed straight for Herbie. Herbie took off like a shot.

The truck chased Herbie around the arena, but Herbie kept speeding up. His lead was getting longer and longer. In a few seconds, Herbie was behind the monster truck and moving up fast!

"I think he's about to whip that guy's tail," Charisma shouted.

The monster truck driver looked in his rearview mirror and saw Herbie on his bumper.

"Hang on, Herbie!" Maggie said as she steered him toward the shell of a wrecked car. She used it as a ramp and launched Herbie toward the monster truck. Herbie hung in the air for a second, and a hundred camera flashes went off.

"Pile driverrrr!" the crowd screamed as Herbie landed hard in the bed of the truck.

"Ha!" The monster truck's driver snorted. "That didn't hurt my truck one bit."

But with a loud crack, the truck's axle snapped, and all four giant tires popped off. The truck's body fell to the mud with a huge crash. The crowd went wild!

Maggie threw her arms around Herbie's wheel, then drove him off the truck bed. He was hers again!

That night on the way to Kevin's garage, Maggie spoke to Herbie. "I'm sorry," she told her battered little car.

Herbie beeped softly as they pulled into the old barn.

Kevin was stunned when he saw Herbie. Maggie climbed out of the car. "I don't care if you never speak to me again," she said to Kevin, "but you have to help Herbie."

She looked down. "I was kind of a jerk, I know."

"Me too," Kevin said to her.

Maggie looked at him. "You weren't a jerk."

"No, I meant *I also know* that you were a jerk," Kevin said, and then he smiled at her. "What about New York and making it big at ESPN?"

Maggie looked at Herbie and nodded. "I met someone who's helping me shift gears. You know, get a better perspective on things."

She looked at Kevin. "Remember that crazy dream we had as kids about being the world's greatest racing team?" she said, and smiled. "I don't think it's so crazy anymore."

Chapter 23

In the Peyton garage at the speedway, car number 86 was up on a lift. Ray was sitting with his headset on. His eyes were closed, and he using a stack of tires as a drum set as he played along with the music. He spun his sticks between beats and raised them in a V when the song ended.

"Thank you, Bangladesh, good night!"

He didn't see Maggie walk in.

"Hey," he yelped, startled and a little embarrassed when she tapped him on the shoulder. He fumbled with the headphones. "I'm kinda nervous about qualifying. I thought you'd be halfway to New York by now."

Maggie looked up at the car. "You're going to be seeing a lot more of me than you thought. Where's Dad?"

Ray motioned to the track. "Walking the

infield. He's pretty tense. You might want to yellow-flag any conversation until after the race."

Maggie was heading out the door when Ray called to her. "You know, sis, you were really great. Sorry you lost. I wish I had half the talent you do behind the wheel."

Maggie turned to him. She was touched by the compliment. "Ray, you're a good driver."

He smiled at her and nodded. "Good doesn't win the cup."

"Dad's never going to give up on you," Maggie said, shaking her head at her father's stubbornness.

"Great," Ray junior said, tossing his drumsticks into the air. "No pressure there. The whole family business is going down the tubes and it's my fault. I never even wanted to race. I wanted to be in a rock band. I've even been writing some songs."

"You should tell him," Maggie said, knowing what it was like to have your *real* dreams denied.

Ray junior wished he could, but he knew better.

"After the way he looked at you yesterday, not a chance."

Maggie nodded and smiled at her brother.

"Good luck," she said as they high-fived. "I'll be pulling for you."

Chapter 24

The next day Maggie and Kevin anxiously waited in the stands for the qualifying race to begin.

The audience cheered as the announcer shouted, "Lots of eager faces in the crowd here to see who will qualify for the few remaining spots in tomorrow's race."

Maggie held her breath as the green flag dropped. This race meant a lot to her family.

"One lap to go for Ray Peyton junior in the number eighty-six car and it's gonna be close," the announcer yelled. Maggie could barely watch.

As Ray miraculously crossed the finish line, Maggie and Kevin jumped up and down, hugging each other.

"He did it! He did it! He did it!" Maggie yelled.

"Holy smokes! Ray Peyton junior has just qualified with a personal best of thirty-eight minutes and fifty seconds," the announcer shouted.

Kevin and Maggie froze as they watched Ray spin out of control and crash into the wall.

They dashed for the parking lot in a panic. It didn't look as if Ray was going to walk away from this one.

(53)

Maggie and Kevin burst into the hospital room. Ray junior was sitting on the edge of the bed. Sally and Ray senior sat in chairs in the corner. Maggie rushed to her brother and gave him a hug.

"You're okay?" she asked Ray anxiously.

"Easy, sis. I'm a little rattled, but all my wiring's still good. Right, Doc?"

Maggie suddenly noticed the doctor in the room. "I'd like to keep you under observation for twenty-four hours," she said to Ray, "but if you want to go, I have no medical reason to stop you."

Maggie turned to her father. "Dad?"

"Not now, Maggie," Ray senior said to her. He nodded at Ray junior. "Come on, son."

Ray junior headed for the door and walked straight into the wall. He reached for the doorknob, but he couldn't seem to find it.

The doctor pulled out a small penlight and turned Ray around. "Ray, follow this light."

She shook her head. "He's lost his depth perception. Could be a problem with his left eye."

"Is it permanent, Doc?" Ray senior asked.

"Well, without further tests it's hard to say. It could come back in an hour. It might never come back. Bottom line: he can't drive tomorrow."

The doctor patted Ray junior on the arm, then left the room. The whole Peyton family was stunned.

"I'm sorry, Dad," Ray junior said.

"It's not your fault," Ray senior said, placing a loving hand on his son's back. "You ran great today."

"I still qualified," Ray junior said hopefully. "If we can find a driver to replace me, we've still got a shot."

He looked at his sister.

Ray senior knew he was thinking about Maggie racing. "That's not going to happen," he said to them both.

Sally walked up to Ray senior and put her hand on his shoulder.

"Ray, if someone doesn't drive tomorrow," she said gently, "Bass Pro's going to drop you, and Team Peyton's racing days will be over. Is that how you want your family legacy to end?"

Old man Peyton dropped his head and walked out of the hospital room.

"Dad!" Maggie called after him. "I'm sorry I lied to you. All I've ever wanted to do is race."

"I'm not putting you behind the wheel of that car," he said to her as they walked down the hospital corridor.

"Why?" Maggie asked. "Because I'm a girl? Because women don't race? I've had one crash. Ray's had dozens."

"It's different," Ray senior answered softly.

"The only difference is he has your support," Maggie argued. "What's really your problem with me racing?"

Ray senior stopped and turned to his daughter. "Because you look just like her, spark plug. You're the spitting image of your mother. I can't lose her twice. I'd rather sell fishing gear for the rest of my life than do that."

Tears welled up in Maggie's eyes. "I may look like her on the outside, Dad, but inside . . . I'm you. I'm a Peyton. Racing's in my blood. I didn't choose it. It chose me. Please, let me drive tomorrow."

"I'm sorry, Maggie," her father said sadly. "I just can't."

Chapter
25

Maggie and Kevin went back to Kevin's garage. Herbie was there. Maggie sighed. The poor car had gone from fully loaded to completely totaled.

"Bad news," Kevin told her after he'd checked his phone messages. "My suppliers won't give me any more parts until I pay off my bills—which are already way overdue."

"So we can't fix up Herbie?" Maggie said, depressed.

"You've got more important things to worry about, sis," Ray junior said, walking into the old barn.

"Shouldn't you be in bed?" Maggie asked, surprised to see him.

Ray junior sat next to his sister. "I'm not blind,

Maggie. I just can't race. But you can, and you're taking my spot tomorrow."

"Whoa! What about Dad?"

"He's always telling me to be a team leader. So I called the rest of the crew. They agree. You're the one."

Maggie threw her arms around Ray. She was thrilled.

"Okay, calm down," Ray said, grinning. "We've got a long night ahead if we're going to have a shot at getting my stock car back in shape."

"There's only one car I'm going to drive, and he's sitting right over there," Maggie said, pointing at the battered car.

"You can't be serious," Ray said.

Kevin looked at his watch. They had only ten hours till race time, and as far as he could tell, they didn't have a car at all.

"I race in Herbie, or I don't race at all," Maggie said firmly.

Ray nodded and hugged his sister. He opened the barn door. A huge semi was backing up to it. It was Ray's pit crew! Team Peyton began unloading every high-tech, high-end tool in the truck: hydraulic jacks, massive pneumatic screwdrivers—the works. Kevin smiled.

"Okay, okay, *okay*," Maggie said, trying to break free. "Let's get to work."

"Come on," Ray called to the pit crew. "We got magic to make!"

Kevin and the pit crew lifted the bent, burnt engine out of the little car with their own hands.

Maggie pulled the rims off his axles and power-bolted on new ones.

Under the car, Ray worked through the night like a surgeon. Finally, a massive engine, shiny as new chrome, was lowered on a winch. Ray, Kevin, and Maggie smiled. Herbie was a work of art, and they were as proud as new parents.

Maggie and Kevin watched as the pit crew spray-painted Herbie a gleaming white. Then Maggie stepped up to the car, held a stencil to the door, and sprayed it blue and red. She peeled it off, revealing a circled number fifty-three.

Herbie was ready!

Chapter
26

The next day, Kevin and Maggie paced anxiously outside the racing official's office. They needed to formally substitute Herbie for Ray's stock car in the race.

Ray burst from the office door, waving an entry form. "Herbie's in!"

In the garage area of the track, a television reporter was interviewing Trip Murphy.

"I'm with Trip Murphy, Cup Series champion," the reporter said. "Trip, the prevailing wisdom in the pressroom is that your only worry today is whether you have enough shelf space for your fourth championship."

"Tell the boys I appreciate the support, but

anything can happen in this sport."

Trip flashed the camera his trademark smile. Then he looked over and his face dropped. Herbie was rolling by, and he'd never looked better.

"We need a moment alone," Maggie told the Team Peyton crew as Herbie rolled into the garage.

The crew looked at her, confused.

"Hey, give the lady some space," Kevin said. They didn't understand, but they left Maggie and Herbie.

Alone in the garage, Maggie kneeled down and spoke softly to the little car. "You nervous?" she asked him.

Herbie beeped.

"It's good to be a little nervous," Maggie said. "It keeps you alert."

She took a deep breath. "In the spirit of honesty, you should know that I did total a car once when I was racing."

Herbie seemed a bit alarmed, but he beeped again confidently.

"Don't worry," Maggie told him. "It was a long time ago. I just wanted to say thanks for not giving up on me."

Herbie gave her a loud and cheerful honk.

"You ready to do this thing?" she said to Herbie. The little car stood up tall on his new tires. "All right. Let's show 'em what we've got."

Chapter
27

Team Peyton escorted Maggie and Herbie onto the track. Maggie couldn't believe it. The stands were filled to capacity with screaming fans.

"Sweetheart, better be careful," someone from the stands yelled. "You're gonna get swatted out there."

But there were lots of believers in the stands too. They'd seen Herbie and Maggie race before.

"You go, girl!" another fan yelled.

Maggie smiled as she climbed into the back of a pickup truck and began her show lap.

The announcers in the booth recognized her.

"Maggie Peyton . . . is that right?" the first announcer said in dismay to the other announcer.

"That's what I've got too," the second announcer said, checking the driver list.

"Okay, Maggie Peyton will be driving the number fifty-three car for Team Peyton. That's Ray Peyton Senior's daughter, I believe."

"And she'll be driving . . . well . . . it says here, a '63 Volkswagen. That's something you don't see every day."

At the Peyton home in Riverside, Ray senior had the TV on. He couldn't believe what he was seeing. There was Maggie waving to the fans at the Speedway.

In the sponsors' area the executives at Bass Pro were stunned to see Maggie as well. "What are you looking at?" Sally asked them. "You've been trying to figure out a way to sell bait and tackle to women for years."

As Maggie passed Trip, she waved politely. He nodded at her and walked over to his brother.

"I checked with the officials," Larry told Trip. "It's all legit. She can race."

Trip was furious. He turned to Crash, who was now wearing a neck brace. "I thought you told me you crushed that car," Trip shouted angrily.

Larry tried to calm his brother down.

"I know you're going to win today, Trip," Larry

said, "but in that microscopic chance that she beats you again, I've lined up a Big-Fat Loser weight-loss campaign."

Trip glared at his brother. Then he gritted his teeth as he watched Maggie step off the lap truck. He walked over and extended his hand.

"Looks like I underestimated you and that car. Good luck today."

"Thanks, Trip," Maggie replied.

Trip smiled warmly.

"Word to the wise: the boys can get pretty rough out there. I heard you had a nasty run-in with a tree back in your street racing days. Wouldn't want a thing like that to shake your confidence."

Trip winked at Maggie and stepped onto the lap truck. Ray junior immediately walked up to Maggie.

"He's just playing head games, Maggie. Ignore him."

Maggie nodded. She agreed with her brother, but she couldn't deny that the remark had rattled her more than a little bit.

Over the PA system, an announcer said, "Ladies and gentlemen, please rise for our national anthem."

Maggie and Herbie were nervous and excited. Maggie put her hand over her heart as Herbie saluted the flag with his windshield wiper.

Charisma was up in the stands between the Hernandez brothers. It was a proud moment for all of them.

As "The Star-Spangled Banner" ended, the crowd cheered and the racing crews jumped into action.

"Let's go, let's go!" Kevin yelled to Team Peyton. "This ain't no street race!"

"Is this what you dreamed it would be like?" Maggie asked, turning to Kevin.

Kevin nodded and replied, "Except all my old teachers would be here. And I'd be in my underwear. The tighty-whitey kind. How about you?"

Maggie laughed and then said wistfully, "Yeah, except I wanted my dad to be cheering me on."

Kevin stared at Maggie. He thought she was beautiful. "There's something I wanted to say," he said to her. Maggie looked at him expectantly. But Kevin became nervous.

"Uh, don't cut your turns too tight," he said.

Maggie shook her head and climbed into Herbie.

"You got it, Chief," she answered. She adjusted her headset as they rolled into position.

"Drivers," the announcer called, "start your engines!" Maggie had thought she'd never hear those words spoken to her.

She started the ignition, and Herbie's engine roared. Forty-two stock cars began to move behind the pace car. Herbie was in the back of the pack. The pace car dropped into the pit and the green flag waved.

"And the race is under way here at the speedway!" the announcer told the crowd.

The stock cars rocketed away. The sound startled Maggie for a second, and she froze.

"Looks like the number fifty-three car got left in the dust," the announcer called.

"Go. Go!" Kevin yelled at her as he held up a handwritten sign that said ACCELERATE!!!

Maggie floored it and took off a split second behind the others. She shifted smoothly into third gear, then fourth. Herbie's tailpipes spit fire as he shot down the track.

"Poor Maggie Peyton in car fifty-three," one of the announcers said. "Looks like her race is over before it even started."

She caught up and passed one driver, then another. But Trip Murphy and most of the pack were way out in front.

Maggie desperately tried to catch up with the pack. "Come on, Herbie," she said, "we're not out of this yet."

From the pit, Kevin was watching with binoculars. He could see Maggie shift into fifth and shoot forward. She was doing one hundred miles per hour. *Stay cool, Maggie*, he thought. *Don't choke.*

Herbie roared up the track. He weaved through the pack, swerving left and right as he passed the other race cars.

Herbie hooked his bumper to the car in front of him and hitched a ride just like Maggie had used to do on her skateboard.

The driver looked behind him. He could see Maggie waving at him. "That little car's riding my bumper," he said into his headset.

"Shake him off," his crew chief ordered into the set.

As the driver came to a turn, Herbie finally shot ahead toward the next pack of cars.

Ray senior was glued to his TV.

"Did you see that move by Maggie Peyton?" an announcer asked, astonished. "Definitely unorthodox, but it put the little lady right back in the race. Bet her granddad's smiling at that one."

A tear came to Ray senior's eye. He looked at the trophy wall. Maybe the Peyton family's days of glory weren't over after all.

Chapter

28

At the speedway, Maggie and Herbie were fighting it out on the ground.

"The temperature inside these cars can heat up to one hundred and twenty degrees," an announcer said as Herbie made his way through the pack. The scoreboard showed that they had raced ninety-six laps.

"Trip Murphy has been in command of this race from lap one," the announcer continued, "but what a comeback story for Team Peyton."

Herbie finally broke ahead of the pack and began to challenge the leaders.

"Ten laps to go in what's shaping up to be one of the most surprising races in racing history. Trip Murphy in number eighty-two has been leading the way, but right now he's feeling the heat from a rookie driving a vintage car for Team Peyton!"

There were only four cars ahead of Herbie now. Maggie made a daring move and overtook two of the cars. She was speeding up to catch Trip Murphy when he dropped his speed and pulled up next to Herbie. Trip smirked as Maggie looked over.

Suddenly, a car swerved toward Herbie from the other side. Herbie lifted onto two wheels, almost flipping. Then the car behind Herbie rammed him so hard that he flew up into a back-end wheelie.

Maggie felt the jolt as Herbie was rammed again and shoved forward. But now, another car was right in front of him. Herbie was completely boxed in.

"Poor Team Peyton," the announcer called out. "Trip Murphy seems bound and determined to take this Cinderella story out of the race."

As Herbie's front tires hit the trunk of the car in front of him, Maggie yelled into her headset, "I'm getting killed out here! I can't shake them!"

Maggie gripped the wheel as Herbie was hit again.

"Yes, you can," the voice over the headset said.

Maggie was startled. "Dad?" she said.

Ray senior was standing next to Kevin in the

pit. "You can, spark plug," Ray senior said. "You can do this."

Maggie clenched her jaw and gripped the wheel confidently.

"So you buckle down and grit your teeth, because you are the next great Peyton, and it's about time everybody knew it!" he shouted into the headset.

"Thanks, Dad."

Maggie mustered up all her courage and did the unthinkable. She gunned the engine and drove over the top of the car ahead of her, doing two hundred miles per hour!

The car behind her spun out of control and took out the car behind it.

"Did you see that?" an announcer yelled. "Tell me you saw that! What an unbelievable move by the fifty-three car! Five laps to go and Maggie Peyton's taken the lead!"

Maggie took a deep breath. Her heart was pounding, but she was back in control.

Kevin, Ray junior, and Ray senior high-fived as Maggie increased her lead.

"Way to go, Maggie!" Kevin cheered.

Suddenly, Maggie sensed a change in Herbie. She glanced at his oil gauge. Sure enough, the oil pressure was dropping.

"We've got a problem," she said into her headset.

Chapter
29

The yellow flag waved from the Peyton pit crew.

"Looks like number fifty-three is leaking oil on the track," one announcer said.

Maggie pulled onto the pit road. Trip Murphy took his first pit stop as well.

"What are you doing?" Crash asked as the crew began changing tires and filling the gas tank. "That little stunt almost cost you the race!"

"Take care of the car; let me worry about the driving," Trip snapped. Crash nodded and checked under the car.

In Team Peyton's pit, Ray junior was rolling out from under Herbie. "Left oil valve cover's cracked," he said to Maggie. "He's leaking bad. I can't fix it in time."

Kevin stepped up. "Tape it, spray it. Fill it with

three quarts of oil," he shouted to the crew, "and pray!"

Everybody froze for a second. "You heard the man," Ray senior said. "Go!"

As the pit crew snapped into action, Kevin leaned over to Maggie. "It may hold for five laps," he said, "it might hold for only one. Either way you've got to avoid being slammed around or else you're going to be out for good."

Maggie nodded. "What do you want to do, Herbie?" she asked. The little car beeped excitedly. He couldn't wait to get back out on the racetrack!

Chapter
30

Trip blurred past Maggie. She was right behind him. Trip looked in his rearview. He saw Maggie tucked in behind his bumper.

"Two laps to go," an announcer called out, "and it's a two-car race! Trip Murphy is clinging to his lead with rookie Maggie Peyton hot on his tail!"

Trip and Maggie rode bumper to bumper, inches apart! But Trip couldn't shake Herbie no matter what he did.

As they zoomed around a corner doing more than two hundred miles per hour, Maggie decided to make her move.

She hit the gas and tried to pass Trip next to the wall. The crowd was going crazy as she pulled up alongside him. But Trip swerved his stock car and rammed Herbie into the wall.

Maggie fought to maintain control as Trip

slammed into her over and over again.

"Maggie," Kevin said into the headset, "Herbie can't take it!" He knew the only thing that was holding the little car together was a piece of duct tape.

At the same time, Crash was yelling at Trip over his headset. "What are you doing? Forget about that car and win the race!"

"He's splatter on my windshield," Trip growled back.

Trip swung wide, then swept back toward Herbie at full speed. Herbie was about to be smashed to bits when Maggie suddenly downshifted. Herbie slowed as Trip zoomed in front of him and straight into the wall.

Trip spun out of control and plowed into two other cars. A devastating pile-up was now in front of Herbie.

Maggie gritted her teeth and accelerated toward the accident.

"Are you ready?" she asked Herbie.

Herbie bravely beeped as they rocketed forward, pinning Maggie to her seat. Herbie was driving full throttle.

Maggie was now only a half mile from the

pile-up and heading for it like a bullet.

Trip was upside down in his stock car, watching Herbie in horror. He screamed just as Herbie veered right. Herbie hit the fence. The stunned crowd gasped as Herbie banked the fence like a stunt bike in a half-pipe. The fence stretched under the force until Herbie was shot back across the track. He made a 360-degree turn through the air, landed on his tires, and shot across the finish line! The crowd went insane in the stands!

"Unbelievable!" an announcer shouted. "I've never seen anything like that in the history of racing. Maggie Peyton has won!"

Chapter
31

Ray senior tousled Kevin's hair. Ray junior was jumping for joy along with Sally and the executives from Bass Pro.

Maggie pulled Herbie into the racetrack's infield. As Herbie came to a stop, she stood up through his sunroof and raised her arms in victory.

The crowd was on their feet, going berserk; the cheering was louder than the revving engines had been!

Maggie spotted her dad and jumped into his arms.

"I'm so proud of you!" Ray senior said to his daughter as he hugged her.

Maggie and her dad turned when they heard a familiar voice.

"I saw him smiling at me!" Trip Murphy was

shouting as his crew carried him away on a stretcher. He was pointing at Herbie. "I'm telling you, that car is alive!"

Herbie beamed as they loaded Trip into an ambulance. "Look," Trip yelled, "he's doing it again!"

"This isn't over!" Trip screamed at Herbie as they were closing the ambulance door. "I'm going to get you! You hear?"

Maggie saw her brother and tossed him one of the hundreds of bouquets that were raining down from the stands. Ray junior caught it with ease. He gave her a wink.

"Wait," Maggie said, her jaw dropping in surprise. "How'd you catch that? I thought your eyes—"

But Ray didn't let her finish.

"The best Peyton was on the track today," he said. "Congrats, sis."

Ray senior walked up to his kids with Sally on his arm. Ray junior looked down and began to shuffle his feet. He knew that his dad had probably seen him catch that bouquet. "Dad, there's something I've got to tell you," he said seriously.

"Is this about your band?" Ray senior asked casually.

Ray junior was shocked.

"I hear you're not bad," his dad said, smiling. "I was thinking maybe we could check them out one night," he said to Sally.

"Ray Peyton, are you asking me on a date?" Sally asked.

Ray senior grinned and gave her a kiss on the cheek.

Maggie smiled too, then noticed Kevin standing alone. She walked over to him.

"You and Herbie make some team," Kevin said, nodding at the little car.

"*We* make some team," Maggie said, grinning at Kevin.

"Yeah," Kevin agreed. "I thought we had a good driver–crew chief rapport out there."

"Herbie," Maggie said, rolling her eyes at Kevin, "you want to help me out here?"

The little car swung his door open and knocked Kevin into Maggie's arms. Kevin looked into her eyes and finally kissed the most beautiful race car driver he had ever known.

The crowd cheered. Herbie's horn blared as his bumper bent into a big smile.

Beep, beep!